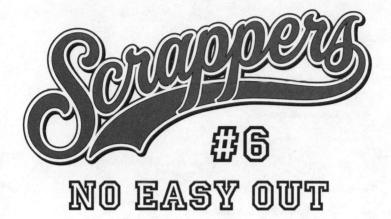

#6
NO EASY OUT

DEAN HUGHES

ATHENEUM BOOKS FOR YOUNG READERS

Atheneum Books for Young Readers
An imprint of Simon & Schuster Children's Publishing Division
1230 Avenue of the Americas
New York, New York 10020

Text copyright © 1999 by Dean Hughes

Also available in an Aladdin Paperbacks Edition.

The text of this book is set in Caslon 540 Roman.

Printed in the United States of America

10 9 8 7 6 5 4 3 2 1

Library of Congress Cataloging-in-Publication Data
Hughes, Dean, 1943-
No easy out / written by Dean Hughes.
p. cm.—(Scrappers #6)
Summary: Adam, a pitcher for the Scrappers, feels a lot of pressure when they have a
shot at the championship, particularly when he has to pitch against his cousin on a rival
team.
ISBN 0-689-81929-3 (hc)   ISBN 0-689-81939-0 (pbk)
[1. Baseball—Fiction. 2. Cousins—Fiction.]
I. Title. II. Series: Hughes, Dean, 1943-   Scrappers 6.
PZ7.H87312Nm   1999   [Fic]—dc21   98-51951

CHAPTER ONE

It was a burning July afternoon. Adam looked up at Mount Timpanogos. A vast snowfield never melted from the deep bowl on the shaded north side of the peak. Right now, Adam Pfitzer wished that's where he was—up there in that cool air and out of the hot spot he had worked himself into in this baseball game.

He took a deep breath and turned his attention back to home plate, where Josh Meyers was waiting. The big guy was swinging his bat, over and over, and he was watching Adam's every move. With runners at first and second, Meyers could tie the game with one swing of the bat.

Adam's team, the Scrappers, had really come together lately. The feeling among the players had been great, and that was showing on the field, too. The Scrappers had finally beaten the

Mustangs—the toughest team in the league—and now they had to keep winning to have a chance at the championship.

Adam knew, though, that he and Ollie Allman, the team's pitchers, were still the biggest worry to the rest of the players. At their best, the two of them were as good as anyone in town, but neither one was consistent.

Adam felt that he had to come through every time he pitched. So the pressure was always on. But his team had gotten off to a good start today against the Hot Rods. The big guns for the Scrappers—Robbie Marquez, Gloria Gibbs, Thurlow Coates, and Wilson Love—had come through in the first inning and pounded out three runs.

But now, in the bottom of the third, after getting the first two batters out, Adam had given up a single to the Hot Rods' left fielder, a guy named Brian Kiesel. Then he had gotten a little too careful with Matt Rohrbach, one of their best hitters. Rohrbach had worked the count full and then walked on a close pitch, barely outside.

Now Adam knew he had to get tough. But when things got tight, he sometimes let his mind wander. Right now he just wanted to think about that snow—about last summer when he and his cousin Stan had hiked the mountain and had taken the wild ride down the glacier, sliding on plastic garbage bags.

Concentrate, Adam told himself silently. He stared at Wilson, who signaled for a fastball. Adam brought his hands to his chest, his glove hiding the ball. He found the strings with his left hand—his pitching hand—and then lined up his fingers on them. He checked the runners.

He reared back, pushed off with his left foot, whipped the ball hard, and followed through as he released it.

His motion was right, and it was a good pitch—not the kind of blinding heater some guys could throw, but at the knees and humming.

Whack!

Meyers met the ball with a perfect stroke and smacked it to right field. Thurlow charged hard, but he had no chance to catch the ball on the fly. He snagged it on one bounce and then *gunned* it home. Kiesel was flying toward the plate, but Thurlow had a cannon for an arm.

The ball was going to be there in plenty of time.

But Wilson glanced to see where the runner was. He took his eye off the ball for just that one moment. The ball hit his mitt but glanced off. By the time Wilson got to the ball, Kiesel had scored and there were runners on second and third.

Adam looked back at the mountain. He knew that he had thrown a good pitch. Meyers had just handled it. Wilson was the one who had messed up, but everyone did at times. Adam wasn't going to waste any time thinking about that.

Jake Oates was coming up now, and he was another big kid. He could sock one out and put the Hot Rods in the lead.

Sometimes Adam wished he didn't play baseball. Sometimes, on summer days, he and Stan rode their bikes to the creek and swam in the cool water. Or they fished the Provo River below the Deer Creek Dam. Swimming, fishing—stuff like that was so much better than all this worry.

"Adam!"

Adam was startled for a moment. He looked

around to see Wilson walking toward him.

"I messed up. We should have been out of the inning," Wilson said. "Just keep throwing the way you have been. We'll be all right. But, hey, pay attention. Okay?" He laughed.

Adam nodded, and he tried to get his mind back where it belonged. "Okay," he said.

Wilson stepped a little closer and said in a softer voice, "Oates is a big swinger. Let's throw him some off-speed stuff and get ahead of him."

So they started with a curveball, but it broke outside and Oates didn't bite. Still, Wilson called for another curve. This time Adam got it over the plate. Oates took a huge cut and fouled the ball into the dirt.

Now Wilson wanted the fastball.

Adam got the ball inside just a little, but Oates hit it off his fists and muscled a little fly into center field.

Jeremy Lim, the Scrappers' center fielder, broke hard toward the infield. It seemed that he would have no chance to get to the ball, but he made up the ground fast. Then he dove, stretched out his upturned glove, and snagged the ball . . . for a moment.

But he couldn't hang on. The ball dribbled out of his glove and into the grass.

Jeremy rolled over in the grass and tried to jump up, but he slipped and fell. Then he had to scramble back to the ball.

Thurlow was running hard to back up Jeremy, but he had a long way to come. Jeremy got to the ball first, spun around, and made a good throw home.

But too late. Both runs scored. The game was tied.

Adam couldn't believe all this had happened with two outs. He hoped the Scrappers' bats would come alive and they wouldn't end up blowing this game.

If they could come back and win, everything would be all right. He imagined himself at the park that night, watching one of the other games. The win would be behind him, the air would be cooling off, and he would feel completely relaxed.

"Adam!"

It was the coach yelling to him.

"We're all right. Just keep your mind on your job."

Adam stepped back to the pitching rubber,

but he didn't want to throw the ball. He was afraid something bad would happen again.

This time, however, he got lucky. He grooved a pitch that David Dietz should have pounded. But the little right fielder chopped the ball straight back to the mound. Adam fielded the ball and flipped it to Ollie on first. The inning was finally over.

As Adam walked to the dugout, he heard a voice in the bleachers. The man wasn't yelling, but he had a loud voice, and Adam heard him clearly. "The pitcher did all right," the man said. "We just need someone out there in center who can catch the ball."

Adam glanced toward the sound and realized it was Mr. Corrigan, Chad's father. Chad would get into the game sooner or later, but right now he was still on the bench. It didn't take a lot of smarts to figure out who Mr. Corrigan thought ought to be playing instead of Jeremy.

But that wasn't fair. Jeremy had made a terrific run and had almost made a great catch.

"Okay," Gloria was shouting. "Let's get some runs. Let's break this game open."

Gloria had been great today. She still liked to give the players on the other team a hard time, but she was being positive with her own players. And it was obvious she liked the leadership she was showing.

Thurlow was yelling, too—and that was really something new. "Everybody hits this inning," he was telling his teammates.

Gloria got her bat and walked to the plate. She was chewing gum, as always, and her uniform was already covered with dirt—for no reason Adam knew of.

"Tag one, Gloria!" Trent Lubak shouted.

She dug in like she meant to do just that. Gloria always had plenty of confidence. What Adam liked now was that *all* of the players were feeling more sure of themselves.

Gloria took the first pitch high for a ball. Rohrbach was pitching. He was throwing hard, as always, and he was getting the ball over the plate most of the time. He didn't change speeds much, or even move the ball around, but the kid could really *bring* the ball.

The next pitch was right there. Gloria unloaded on it.

She hit a bullet to left that was . . .

Smack!

Eric Fellows, the shortstop, leaped in the air and caught it.

Fellows tossed the ball back to Rohrbach, and then he took his glove off and looked at his hand. Adam knew the guy's palm was stinging. Gloria had hit the stuffing out of the ball.

"Oh, man," Adam moaned. "When are we going to get a break?"

Ollie was sitting next to him on the bench. "We should be way ahead now, not tied. They lucked out to get their runs, and we haven't had a break yet."

Gloria tossed her batting helmet toward the fence, and then she trotted down to the water fountain. Adam knew she was working hard not to show her frustration.

Thurlow was up now. He held off on the first pitch, but the umpire called it a strike.

"I've got to keep my head in this game," Adam said. "I keep thinking about being up on the mountain—or swimming in the creek."

"That's not so bad. Go ahead and think about that stuff. It'll calm you down. The coach always says it's better not to think too much about your motion as you throw the ball."

Adam thought maybe that was right. "Give it a ride, Thurlow," he shouted, and he clapped his hands.

"Just don't space out—and forget what planet you're on," Ollie said.

Adam laughed, but he knew that's how other kids thought about him. He also knew they weren't exactly wrong. Sometimes he did get a little lost in space. What he really wished was that he could be the guy to lead his team to victory—the guy everyone knew they could rely on.

Thurlow connected on the next pitch and drove the ball to left field. For a moment, Adam thought it might get out of the park. But it was too high. Kiesel ran back, got under it, and hauled it in.

Wilson was up after that. He took a couple more pitches, then cracked a shot to right. But the right fielder didn't have to move. He just stood his ground and watched the ball sail into his glove.

Three up, three down. And Adam had to go to work again.

"You're getting good wood on the ball," Coach Carlton yelled to the players as they took the field again. "Don't worry. The hits will start to drop in. Let's go get 'em out again."

As Adam took the mound, he heard his teammates yelling for him, cheering him on. But in the Hot Rods' dugout, the players were all hollering, "Pfitzer doesn't have anything. We can hit him." The noise all seemed to mix together, and it was annoying. Adam tried to shut it out.

He looked up at the snowfield, took a breath, and tried to feel the calm. He remembered skiing the winter before at Sundance, a ski resort, just below that peak. It had been his third season skiing, and he had finally been able to relax and enjoy the good ride. He tried to remember the gentle shoosh of the powder as he got ready to throw.

Bam! He shot a rocket at Ricky Tobias. Tobias seemed surprised by the speed. He didn't trigger, and the ump called the pitch a strike.

Adam glanced away, took a breath, and fired another pitch that was just as hot. Tobias swung and missed this time.

So Adam stayed with his fastball, and he threw a perfect one over the outside edge. Tobias took an awkward swing and missed again.

Strike three.

This felt good. Adam got a ground-ball out after that, then another strikeout, and he was heading back to the dugout. He liked the calm, and he really believed his teammates were about to bust loose.

But Tracy Matlock and Trent both hit fly balls for outs. Adam came up to bat thinking that he needed to get something started himself.

The first pitch was belt high, and Adam pasted it. The ball darted toward left center, and Adam was sure it would go for extra bases. But the center fielder could really rocket. He chased after the long fly and made the grab.

Adam was heading back to the mound already.

Something had to give before much longer. The game was going to the bottom of the fifth, and the score was still 3 to 3.

CHAPTER TWO

Adam looked good in the fifth, but he made one bad pitch. He got the ball in Kiesel's power zone, and the kid cranked it over the left field fence.

Adam hated to fall behind late in the game, and he felt the nervousness again. But in the top of the sixth, Robbie knocked a long drive for a triple. Then Thurlow drove a fly to the fence for a double, and Robbie scored. But Wilson flew out, and the Scrappers only got one run.

Adam could only think how close Thurlow had come to hitting a homer, and that his team could have been ahead now. But with the score tied, he still believed his teammates would come through with some more runs in the seventh. All he had to do was get six more outs.

After Adam took his warm-up pitches, Wilson

crouched down, popped his fist into his mitt, and then shouted to the infield, "Let's go, Scrappers. Three up, three down!"

Adam gazed off at the mountain for a few seconds. Then he shut his eyes and tried to feel some of the steadiness and firmness that he saw. Gloria yelled to him, "You're doing great, Adam. Just keep it up." He liked that. She meant it, he could tell, and he knew that he had pitched pretty well today.

Still . . . he wished that the game were over and that the Scrappers had the win.

Adam looked to Wilson for a sign. Curve. He nodded. Then he threw a good pitch that was over the plate but dropping away from the batter.

Dietz was obviously looking for a fastball. He swung early, but he did manage to make contact and bounce the ball down the first base line. Ollie ran forward, took the ball on a high hop, then stepped in front of Dietz and tagged him out.

"One pitch, one out!" Wilson shouted. "That's it, Adam. Two more!"

A girl Adam knew from school—Angela

Hobart—stepped into the batter's box. She was in the game as a sub for Ricky Tobias. She was a left-handed batter and a pretty good athlete—no Gloria, but pretty good.

Adam rocked and fired. There was no trickery this time—just a good ol' fastball. She swung under it and lifted it straight in the air.

"Mine, mine!" Wilson shouted. He stripped off his mask, then brought up his mitt to shield his eyes from the bright sunlight. The big guy staggered a little as he got under the ball, but he reached up and made the catch.

"Two away," shouted Wilson, and he flipped the ball to Adam. "One more."

The other Scrappers were all telling Wilson, "Nice catch!"

Another of the Hot Rods' subs stepped to the plate—a kid who looked a little scared. Adam loved the way he felt. The game was on the line, but he was staying in control of his worries. He was throwing about as well as he ever had.

He tossed a gunshot of a fastball, and the little batter looked terrified. Adam came down the middle with two more fireballs, and the batter never moved.

"Strike three!" the ump shouted. Wilson tossed the ball on the grass and ran back to the dugout.

Adam didn't run. He walked confidently. Now, in the top of the seventh, it was time for his team to come through. Then he would get those last three outs.

The Scrappers' fans were screaming, and Adam glanced up at his big sister—a good softball player—who was waving and smiling. Adam's dad was there, too, but he was a quiet guy. He nodded to Adam and smiled.

Cindy Jones was in the game now for Tracy, and she was up to bat first. She was one of the Scrappers who had been improving over the past few weeks. She was no power hitter, but she was starting to stroke the ball.

After working the count full, Cindy poked one over the second baseman's head, just beyond his reach.

The Scrappers whooped it up. Cindy had come through, and that brought up Chad, who was in the game for Trent. He was the ninth batter. If he could stay alive, all the best hitters would be coming up.

"Come on, Chad!" a voice from the bleachers bellowed. It was Chad's father again. "Show 'em now. Bring that run home."

Adam couldn't believe anyone had a voice that loud.

Chad took a couple of pitches for balls, and his dad kept the thunder rolling. "Way to watch 'em, Chad!"

"I'm glad that's not my dad," Tracy whispered to Adam. "I'd be *so* embarrassed."

All the Scrappers were glancing at one another and trying not to laugh.

The next pitch looked good. Chad flicked his bat at it. It was an awkward swing, but it connected. The ball arced like a rainbow and dropped into short left field.

"That's the way! That's the way!" Mr. Corrigan roared. The Scrappers all laughed. But they were cheering, too.

Cindy had to stop at second. But that was all right. Two on, no one out, and Adam was coming up. He felt sure that the Scrappers' big inning was finally going to happen.

Adam let a pitch go by, but then he jumped on a fastball and drove it hard to the left side. It looked like a sure single, but Fellows dove to his left and snagged the ball—took it right out of the air for the out.

Cindy had begun to break for third, and a good throw might have caught her off base. But she dove back safely before Fellows could scramble to his feet.

Adam couldn't believe his bad luck again, but the Scrappers were still all right. Ollie was coming up, and he could get the job done.

Things took a better turn, too. Rohrbach tried to be too careful with Ollie. He ended up walking him, and now the bases were loaded with Robbie and Gloria coming up.

"Do it now, Robbie," Adam shouted. "Bring 'em all in!"

Robbie didn't waste any time. He slammed the first pitch into left field. The only problem was, he hit it almost too hard. It got to the left fielder quickly. He picked it up on one bounce and made a good throw back to the infield. Cindy scored, but Chad, who was pretty slow, had to hold up at third.

At least the Scrappers had the lead. Now Gloria could break the game open.

Gloria did hit a hard shot, but it was a bouncer up the middle, heading for center field.

Adam jumped up. He expected to see two runs score. But Fellows darted to his left and stabbed the ball. His momentum carried him straight to second base. He stepped on the bag and then fired to first.

"*Out!*" the umpire screamed.

It was impossible. The Hot Rods had gotten out of the inning and had only given up one run. And *Gloria* had been caught in a double play.

For a moment, no one believed it, but then the Scrappers began grabbing their gloves.

"That's all right," they were yelling. "All we need is three outs."

That's what Adam told himself, too. The Scrappers were up 5 to 4, and he was sure he could hold the lead. But he wasn't quite so calm as he had been the last couple of innings.

Kevin Banks was coming up first. He was the ninth batter and not a great hitter. Adam put a fastball in a perfect spot: over the outer edge of the plate. But Banks reached out and hit it off the end of his bat. The ball spun toward Tracy at second and then took a crazy hop to her right. It skipped off her glove and hit her shoulder, then rolled away.

Tracy hustled, but by the time she picked up the ball, she didn't have a chance to get Banks at first.

Some of Adam's composure seemed to slip away. All the luck was running one way today, it seemed. He looked at the mountain again, tried to draw in the peace he had felt before. But his stomach was rolling.

He hated to see Fellows coming up, but Adam had struck him out twice already today. He could do it again.

The first pitch was down the middle, but Fellows wasn't swinging. Adam knew he was hoping for a walk. So Adam came hard with another fastball in the strike zone. Fellows was still taking, and now the count was 0 and 2.

Wilson set the target inside. Adam knew that Fellows had a tendency to bail out, so that seemed the perfect strikeout pitch: inside corner with some mustard on the pitch.

But Adam tried to aim the ball, and he didn't get much on it. It was off the plate, too far inside.

Fellows started to bail out, and then he

seemed to see his opportunity. He leaned his hip forward and let the ball hit him.

"Take your base," the ump called, and he pointed to first.

"Come on, ump," Gloria yelled. "He did that on purpose!"

Adam didn't want her to explode—the way she did sometimes—so he trotted toward home himself. "Sir," he said to the umpire, "the batter leaned into the pitch. He has to try to get out of the way, or—"

"I know the rule. But that's not how it looked to me. Just go back and pitch."

Adam didn't want to cause a lot of trouble, but this was wrong. "Ask the other umpire," he said.

The home plate ump pointed to the umpire in the infield, but the guy out there shook his head.

"Satisfied now?" the umpire asked.

"No, sir, I'm not," Adam answered, but he turned and walked back to the mound.

When he got there, Robbie was waiting for him. "Forget it," Robbie said. "There's nothing you can do about it now. Just mow these next three guys down. You've done it before; you can do it again."

"All right," Adam said. He wiped his forehead with the palm of his hand. Gloria was mumbling and kicking dirt, but at least she hadn't erupted. Still, Adam felt the tension.

Kiesel was up again, and he was tough. Adam took the sign from Wilson and fired a hard fastball that was up and away. Kiesel reached out for it and hit a little blooper toward left field.

Chad had been playing up, and he got a great jump. He charged hard and dove for the ball.

Adam was running to back up home plate, in case the ball dropped. For a moment, he wasn't sure what had happened. But then Chad jumped to his feet and held his glove in the air.

Finally, a break. Chad was not a great player, but he had made a great catch.

A sound like a jet engine came out of the stands—a huge cry of joy from Mr. Corrigan. And then he shouted, "*All right*, Chad! Great play!"

Everyone else in the bleachers—and most of the players, too—laughed at the enormous reaction. Chad just ducked his head and trotted back to his position in left. Adam came back to the mound feeling a whole lot better. But Rohrbach was coming up. The guy could hit the ball a mile. Adam wound up and delivered a strong fastball. Rohrbach took the strike.

Adam thought he should throw nothing but heat, but Wilson signaled for a change-up. Maybe that wasn't a bad idea. They might as well keep the big guy off balance.

Rohrbach was thrown off, all right, but he stuck his bat out late.

The ball clicked off the bat and arced toward right field, where Martin Epting was now playing.

Thurlow might have gotten to it, but Martin couldn't.

When the runner on second saw that the ball was going to drop, he took off hard. Martin came to a stop and let the ball roll to him, then made a weak throw.

And the run scored easily.

Adam couldn't believe it. A little blooper of a hit had tied the game. Rohrbach was loving it, too. He was acting like he had hit a line drive.

But the game wasn't lost. Adam had to remember that. He knew he couldn't let himself get upset. All his teammates were cheering for him, and he knew he had good stuff today.

The next batter—Meyers—was another powerhouse. But Adam threw well. He had Meyers 1 and 2 and was looking for the strikeout. But he let a fastball sail on him a little, and Meyers cracked a hard shot to center.

Adam spun around—frightened—but then he saw that the ball was heading straight at Jeremy. No problem.

Jeremy hardly had to move. He just stood his ground, stuck his glove up, and pulled the ball in . . . and then dropped it.

Adam had started to turn away when suddenly the ball was on the ground. Jeremy scrambled after it and made the throw, but too late.

The Hot Rods had won the game, 6 to 5.

CHAPTER THREE

The Scrappers were stunned. They gathered around Coach Carlton, all silent. "That was a tough one," he told them. "You outhit them, outfielded them, outpitched them. You did all the right things. We had some errors that hurt us, of course, but mostly, they got lucky. That's just the way it goes some days."

"Coach," Adam said, "Fellows leaned into my pitch. If the ump hadn't called that wrong, we would have won."

"I know. I agree. But that's part of the game. Umpires are going to make bad calls sometimes. We've got the Stingrays on Thursday. Let's start thinking about that."

"We're going to have to play a lot better than we did today," Gloria said.

"That's true, Gloria," the coach said. "But I

don't want anyone worrying about the mistakes we made in this game. Those things happen to the best players."

Gloria ducked her head and didn't say anything. Adam knew she was upset about Jeremy's error, but she was trying not to show it.

Adam glanced at Jeremy. He was looking down at the grass. Adam could see that it was all he could do not to cry. There was no way he was going to walk away and forget about a mistake as big as that one.

As the kids began to leave, the coach headed toward Jeremy, but as he passed Chad, he put his hand on Chad's shoulder and said, "That was a good catch you made, Chad."

Mr. Corrigan was standing close by. "It was a *great* catch," he said. Then he walked to the coach. "He's ready for some more playing time, don't you think, Coach?"

"He's done well lately. That's why he's playing more than he did early in the season."

Adam could tell that the coach didn't know what to say. He could also see that Chad was really embarrassed.

Mr. Corrigan lowered his voice—but not

much—and said, "If that short little kid in center is gonna drop fly balls like that, why isn't Chad in there for him? That boy cost us the game."

Coach Carlton stiffened. "Jeremy has saved us a lot of times this summer, Mr. Corrigan." The coach looked toward Jeremy, who was now walking away. "Just a minute, Jeremy," Coach Carlton called to him. Then he followed him, and the two talked, quietly.

Adam felt bad for Jeremy, but he felt just as bad for Chad. The poor guy was pleading with his dad to lay off, but his dad was still talking way too loud, and he told Chad, "Hey, you deserve to be out there."

Adam had planned to go to his cousin's game that night, but after what happened in his own game, he didn't feel like it. Later on, though, he called Stan, who played for the Pit Bulls. Early in the season, Stan had spent most of his time on the bench, but Scott Johnson had fallen while in-line skating and had broken his arm. That had given Stan a chance to be the starting second baseman.

When Stan heard Adam's voice on the phone, the first thing he said was, "I heard you guys lost today. How did that happen?"

Adam told him the story, and then he asked, "How did your game come out?"

"Okay. We won."

"Then how come you sound like you lost?"

Adam had taken the cordless phone from the family room, and he had it in his bedroom. He was lying on his bed, looking up at the ceiling, where he had tacked a Mark McGwire poster. Even though he was a pitcher, he had always wished he were a big slugger like McGwire.

"I went 0 for 4. I just can't seem to get a hit," Stan said. "I'm worried that my coach is going to put me on the bench again if I don't start doing better."

"Sometimes the hits just don't drop in. I wouldn't worry about it," Adam said.

"It's worse than that. I'm not connecting. Something is all wrong with my swing. I'm striking out a lot."

"Everyone has slumps." Adam got up from his bed and headed downstairs to the kitchen, but he was still holding the phone to his ear. He was thirsty, and he wondered whether any sodas were left in the refrigerator.

"Maybe I'm just not that good," Stan said. "The pitchers are a lot better in this league than they were in the younger leagues. Maybe I can't cut it at this level."

"Come on, Stan. Don't be so tough on yourself." It had been Adam's dad's turn to clean up after dinner that night. He had finished, and the dishwasher was running, but he was sitting at the kitchen table with the newspaper in front of him.

"If you want, I'd be happy to throw to you," Adam told Stan. "Maybe you just need a little extra practice."

"Yeah, I might take you up on that." But Stan didn't sound like he thought it would help. Adam could tell that he was even more discouraged than he wanted to admit.

"All right. Let me know."

"Yeah. Anyway, sorry about your game. Was everyone pretty mad at Jeremy?"

"No. Not at all. I don't know what happened. The ball hit his glove, and then it just popped out."

"Hey, that's happened to me before."

"I know. It's happened to all of us. I think Jeremy would have been all right if Chad Corrigan's dad hadn't started mouthing off." And then Adam told Stan about the incident with Mr. Corrigan. By then he had found a two-liter bottle of soda in the refrigerator. As he talked, he got out an ice tray from the freezer, and he found his big Utah Jazz drinking cup.

When Adam finally said good-bye to Stan, he had poured his drink. He was putting the bottle back in the refrigerator when his dad said, "Aren't you playing against Stan's team pretty soon?"

"Yeah. Next week," Adam told him.

"Will you be pitching that game?"

Adam had to think. "Probably. That should be my turn."

So far, Adam had not ended up pitching to Stan in a game. He wasn't sure how he would feel about that. He knew how much it meant to Stan to start hitting better. Adam hated to think he could be the guy making him look bad.

"Would the kids on your team like it if they saw you practicing with him?"

"I don't know. I hadn't thought about that." And suddenly he was a little worried. Maybe the players would think he wasn't being loyal to his own team.

"They *shouldn't* care," his dad said. "But some kids take sports way too seriously."

"Stan's been having a hard time, Dad. He's probably not going to knock a homer and beat us. So I don't see why anyone should care."

Mr. Pfitzer was a tall man, and thin. He leaned back now and stretched out his legs under the table. "I agree, Adam. I'm glad you look at it that way. Your uncle Richard was telling me the other day how much Stan envies you—because you're better at sports than he is. So if you can give him some help, I think you should."

"It's no big deal. I'll just throw him some pitches."

"But then, what about the game? What will you do then?"

"I don't know. Strike him out if I can. He's still on the other team."

"Yeah. That's right. That's what you have to do. But after you play each other, you might give him some extra help."

"I don't want him to be *too* good, Dad. We have to play them again."

"But he's your cousin—and your good friend. Teach him all you can."

But Adam wondered about that. What if players on his own team saw him working out with Stan all the time? Would they think he was being disloyal?

The Scrappers practiced the next morning. Adam threw a few easy pitches, just to loosen his arm, but mostly he worked on his infield play and his hitting.

Adam noticed that Jeremy was still feeling bad. He was even quieter than usual. At least Chad seemed to go out of his way to be friendly to him.

When practice was over, Adam and Wilson were standing by the bat rack, talking. The coach was putting the bats away when Chad walked up to him. Adam heard Chad say, "Coach, I'm sorry about yesterday. You know, all the stuff my dad was saying."

"Don't you worry about that," Coach Carlton said. "He was just sticking up for you."

"Yeah, but I don't hear the other guys' dads saying stuff like that. It made me feel pretty stupid."

"Can you tell him what you just told me?"

"I don't know. Maybe. He gets worked up sometimes. He's got his mind all made up that I should be in center instead of Jeremy. But I don't feel that way."

Chad glanced toward Adam and Wilson. They both looked away and then began talking to each other.

"Don't worry about it, Chad," Coach said. "Your dad is right about one thing. You've improved a lot. If we're going to have any chance to win the championship, our bench will have to come through. You're just as important as the starters."

"I don't mind being a sub. I didn't play much baseball before this year. I'm just getting so I really like it."

"Tell me this. Do *you* feel like I've treated you fairly?"

"Sure." Chad's head came up. "You've been great. You work with me all the time, and you let me play every game. That's what I told my dad."

Coach Carlton smiled. "Well, fine, then. Let's not worry about it. I might have to tell your dad to back off a little if he talks about the other players. But other than that, I have no problem."

"Okay. I told him to lay off about Jeremy, but I don't know if he will."

Chad glanced at Adam again, and this time Adam gave him a nod. He wanted him to know that the other players weren't blaming Chad for the things his dad had said.

The next day's practice was much more intense. And the coach put the situation on the line. "We have to take one game at a time," he said, "but to have a chance at the second-half championship, we have to play every game like it's for all the marbles. That means we can't ease up just because we're playing the Stingrays. We've beaten them twice before, but they'll be coming after us this time."

Adam rode his bike home after practice, and Ollie rode along with him. Adam had something he wanted to ask Ollie, but he wasn't sure where to start. "The way the schedule works out, I guess I'll be pitching against the Pit Bulls," he said first.

"Yeah. I'm glad I got the Stingrays. They don't scare me as much."

"My cousin Stan plays for the Pit Bulls. Lately, he's been starting, but he's not getting any hits."

"He's not that good, is he?"

"I don't know. I always thought he was pretty good at sports. But he's not doing very well this year. I feel sorry for him."

"Just don't feel sorry for him when you pitch to him. Blow him away, cousin or not. Then after the game, you can tell him what he did wrong." Ollie laughed.

"My dad wants me to work with him and try to help him improve. Do you think I should do that?"

"I don't know. What if he starts cracking lots of hits and beats us sometime?"

"That's what worries me."

"Maybe you should just give him a few pointers—the kind of stuff coaches always say— and then let it go at that."

"Yeah. Maybe so."

But after, Adam wondered about that. Maybe he should help Stan as much as he could and then do everything he could to strike him out in a game. That seemed fair enough. But he still wondered what his teammates would think. If Stan started doing better, they might think Adam was going easy on him.

CHAPTER FOUR

The next day was game day, and the temperature was still sizzling in Wasatch City. But the Scrappers were ready to play. All the players believed that they still had a shot at the championship, and they were mad about their hard-luck loss to the Hot Rods.

It was time to *kick* someone and serve notice to the rest of the league that the Scrappers were coming on strong.

Ollie was pitching today, and that meant that Adam would be starting at first. Adam had his mind made up that he wanted to hit better today. That was a way he could contribute more to the team. But there was another thought in the back of his mind. He wanted Ollie to know—absolutely—that he wasn't giving anything to anyone, that he was playing all out for the Scrappers. Ollie needed to know where Adam's loyalties were.

What Adam wished was that he had never mentioned the situation with Stan.

Ollie looked good during his warm-up pitches. He was still mumbling to his glove, the ball, himself—or something. His lips were moving all the time, but he was keeping his voice down, and whatever he was saying seemed to be working. He was throwing hard, without forcing the ball, and he was getting the ball over the plate.

Petey Peterson was leading off for the Stingrays. He was a gritty little player. He dug in, held his bat high, and gave Ollie a hard stare.

Thump!

Ollie's first pitch hit Wilson's mitt with a smack. Adam saw the surprise on Wilson's face. Ollie had thrown a missile.

Petey backed out of the box and seemed to think things over. The kid looked scared when he stepped back in.

But Petey didn't let the next pitch go by. He

lashed at the ball, got a whole lot of nothing, and almost fell down. Adam laughed out loud.

Ollie finally wasted a curve outside, but then he came back to his hot stuff. Petey started to swing, tried to stop, and ended up chopping the ball toward Gloria. The ball was moving slowly, and Peterson was pretty quick. Adam got to the bag, set his feet, and waited.

Gloria charged the ball, picked it up on the run, and then fired a shot that almost took Adam's glove off.

Gloria was psyched. That was obvious. Ollie's pitching had everyone excited, but Gloria's throw was like putting a match to dynamite. The Scrappers were all talking it up now, yelling to one another, feeling their power.

The next batter, a girl named Elise Harris, seemed a little unsure of herself as she stood in the box. She was obviously feeling the Scrappers' energy. But she hung tough, took a good swing at a hard fastball, and drove a fly to center.

Jeremy jogged back a few steps and gauged the distance just right. Then he reached up with both hands and put the squeeze on the ball.

He had been extra careful, but he made the

catch the way the coach always taught the kids to do it. Adam heard Chad holler from the dugout, "Way to go, Jeremy! Nice catch."

What Adam didn't hear was any noise from Mr. Corrigan.

Michael Reynolds, the Stingrays' star player, tried to look confident when he stepped in next, but Adam thought he fussed around longer than usual as he got set, and he was squeezing the bat handle like he wanted to strangle it.

Ollie popped a fastball in tight, and Reynolds was quick to spin away. Ball one.

Ollie spun a curve then, and it was a beauty. But Reynolds stayed with it. He stuck his bat out and poked the ball to the right side. It was gliding into shallow right field—and was going to fall in for a base hit.

But then . . . there was Thurlow.

The guy was running like a racehorse. He dove—laid himself out completely—and picked off the ball just before it hit the grass.

He jumped up and held the ball in the air, and the umpire shouted, "Out!"

The top of the inning was over.

Adam ran for Thurlow. "That was *amazing!*"

he yelled. "We came to play! Don't get in our way today." He gave Thurlow a high five, and then he ran for Ollie. "You're on fire, Ollie. If you're talking to the ball, you're saying all the right stuff."

"I'm talking to my hands today. And my right elbow sometimes." Ollie seemed to mean it, too.

Adam laughed. "All I know is, you've got the Stingrays talking to their toes. They were all looking down when they walked away."

The Scrappers charged into the dugout to get set up for their first at bat. The place was electric with excitement. When Jeremy walked out to the plate, Trent yelled, "We *all* hit this inning. Every one of us."

Adam liked that, but he felt the pressure, too. On days when he was pitching, he figured he would be okay if he just tossed a good game. But today, he wanted to be a big part of the offense, and he hadn't done that for a while.

Bullet Bennett wasn't pitching for the Stingrays today. The pitcher was a hefty kid named Jon Jackson. There was no question he could throw the ball hard, but as Adam watched him warm up, it didn't look like he did anything but try to get it over the plate with some speed on it.

Jeremy wasted no time getting the rally started. Jackson threw a good fastball, but Jeremy punched a line drive between first and second. Then, when he saw the right fielder take his time getting to the ball, Jeremy darted toward second and got there standing up.

It was an aggressive play, and the Scrappers erupted all over again. This was their day, and everyone seemed to know it.

Robbie was ready. He slapped a line drive into the left field corner for a double, and Jeremy scored. Just like that, the Scrappers were on the board.

Gloria was so fired up she could hardly stand still at the plate, but when Jackson threw her one of his fastballs over the heart of the plate, she jumped at it and knocked a long shot to left. The left fielder probably should have had it, but he didn't get a good jump—and wasn't all that fast. The ball dropped beyond his glove and rolled to the fence.

Gloria ended up with a triple, and Robbie scored. Two to nothing.

Jackson was so mad he looked like he was ready to throw *at* Thurlow, not to him. But he had to be worried, too. Two doubles and a triple, and now the power hitters were coming up.

Thurlow might have been a little too eager to paste one over the fence. He swung hard and almost missed a pitch. The ball dropped off his bat and rolled down the third base line.

Reynolds charged from third and grabbed the ball. But Thurlow was just too fast. There was no chance to get him.

Reynolds spun and looked for Gloria, but she had played it smart and stayed at third. Thurlow was safe at first, and now there were runners at first and third, Wilson coming up, and still no outs.

Wilson took that strange, clumsy stance of his, and he waited. He took a strike at the knees, without swinging.

Robbie had sat down next to Adam by then. "He wants something up where he can drive it," Robbie said. "He'd like to knock one out of here."

"He's due to get one, too," Adam said.

Wilson let another pitch go by, this one a ball, too low.

"Ollie told me that your dad wants you to help your cousin with his hitting."

"Yeah."

"Are you going to do it?"

"I'll pitch to him—and give him some pointers. That won't hurt anything, will it?"

"I guess not."

Wilson laid off another pitch that seemed to be down and in. The umpire called it a strike.

"Don't you think I should?" Adam asked.

"I don't know. Some of the players are worried you might go easy on him in a game—maybe let him get a hit."

"I wouldn't do that."

"I know. But if people see you working out together, they might get the wrong idea."

"They ought to know I wouldn't do that."

"Maybe so. But some of them are wondering."

Wilson finally got what he was looking for: a fastball at the letters. He took a mighty swing but only produced a duck of a fly ball. Still, it was a duck that knew where to land. It dropped over the shortstop's head for another hit.

Gloria scored, and Thurlow had to stop at second. Three runs in and still no outs. Adam wondered why the hits hadn't dropped like this when he had pitched.

But Adam could hardly think about the game right now. "Robbie, you know I wouldn't do that. Don't you?"

"Sure. But maybe you shouldn't even try to help him—at least until the season is over."

Maybe that was right. But what could Adam tell his dad?

When Tracy knocked a line-drive single, Thurlow scored.

Adam had to go out to the on-deck circle, and he had to get focused on the game again.

Trent lifted a fly ball into center, and it seemed that Jackson was finally going to get an out.

But the center fielder was staring at the sky, looking confused. It was obvious he had lost the ball in the sun. Suddenly he ducked and covered his head, and the ball dropped on the grass directly in front of him. He picked it up and

made a pretty good throw to second, but Tracy
had seen what was coming. She had broken toward second before the ball dropped, and she
slid in safely.

The bases were loaded now, and Adam was
up. But he was still upset. His teammates already thought he was strange. He didn't want
them to think he was less than one hundred percent committed to the team.

"Come on, Adam, keep it going," Robbie
was yelling. "We're going to hit around. No one
makes an out."

"I want another chance to hit a homer this inning," Wilson shouted from third base.

It was all sort of fun—and funny—but Adam
was serious. He wanted to get a hit more than he
ever had before.

The look on Jackson's face was scary. The
guy had massive shoulders and powerful arms.
Adam set up in the batter's box and ground his
rear foot into the dirt. He held his bat high and
waved it in a little circle.

Jackson took his sign from the catcher, nodded, and then he pumped a hard one down the
middle. Adam saw it all the way and took an

enormous swing. But he swung under the ball and fouled it back to the screen.

Adam focused on Jackson again. He had something he had to prove.

The next pitch was fast but at the belt, and Adam watched it all the way. He didn't swing hard; he merely stroked the ball. When he hit it, though, he knew he had gotten all of it. He felt that clean, hard contact all the way up his arms.

The ball shot off his bat toward left, and it just kept going. It sailed high and long—longer than any ball he had ever hit. He trotted toward first, but he couldn't take his eyes off the ball. It was like something Thurlow would hit—a *monster* of a shot.

Grand slam!

The Scrappers were up 8 to 0, and Adam had just hit his first home run of the season. But he felt hungry, almost angry, as he charged around the bases. He wanted to keep pouring on the runs. He wanted everyone to see that he was one of the scrappiest of the Scrappers, that he was out there leading his team, not just going along for the ride.

CHAPTER FIVE

"Now let's play some defense," Coach Carlton called to his players as they grabbed their gloves and headed back to the field. The first inning was finally over, and the Scrappers had scored a total of ten runs. If they could hold that lead past the third inning, they would win the game automatically, according to the "mercy rule" in the league.

But things quieted down for the next two innings, and the Scrappers didn't score again. Meanwhile, the Stingrays managed to get a run when big Elvin Badger clouted a triple off Ollie and then scored on an infield out.

Coach Carlton had made some early changes by then. He asked Cindy to play second base for Tracy, and he put Chad in right field. Thurlow had moved to center, so Jeremy was out of the game. Now, as the fourth inning began, Martin had taken over for Adam at first base.

As the Scrappers took the field, Adam sat by Tracy and Jeremy. He didn't like having to sit around, and he hadn't wanted to leave the game, but he loved having the big lead.

Ollie got a couple of outs, but then he gave up a single and a walk. Adam hoped he wasn't losing his concentration. Jackson was up to bat. He was a powerful kid and not used to being shown up the way he had been on the mound today. Adam knew the guy was looking to knock one out of the park and save a little pride.

But Jackson was a cocky kid, and it was good to see him brought down a little. Ollie threw a curve, and Jackson must have been expecting a fastball. He made an awkward stab at the ball and missed.

"Way to go," Adam yelled to Ollie. "Keep him off balance."

Just then Adam heard someone say, "Ollie is looking *tough* today."

Adam looked around and saw his cousin Stan, who was standing behind the fenced-off dugout area. Adam wasn't sure he wanted Stan to be there, but he said, "When Ollie has his control, he's tough all right."

"What's wrong with Jackson today?" Stan asked.

"He's not that great. He throws hard, but anybody can hit a fastball if that's all a pitcher throws."

"Maybe 'anybody' can, but I can't. Jackson struck me out three times the last time we played those guys."

Adam realized he had said the wrong thing, and he felt sorry for Stan. "Well . . . you know . . . I'm not saying he isn't good. I just meant that speed isn't everything."

Stan nodded. He watched, and so did Adam, as Jackson took an inside pitch for a ball.

"Well, anyway, our game is right after yours. Do you want to go swimming or something after my game?" Stan sounded sort of down. Maybe he was just nervous.

Adam thought he probably ought to spend some time with Stan, but he wasn't sure he wanted to. Stan had always been his best friend, but this new situation had become uncomfortable. Still, he said, "Yeah. Sure. Let's go down to our swimming hole." That was a fairly private place, where not a lot of kids would see them.

"Okay. Good." Stan suddenly looked a lot happier. He watched as Jackson took a wild swing at another off-speed pitch. "Ollie *is* on today," he said. "I'll see you later."

Jackson finally got wood on a pitch. He drove a high fly to right field. Chad had plenty of time to drop back and get under the ball. When he made the catch, Mr. Corrigan shouted, "That's the way to haul 'em in out there, Chad. Great play! Great play!"

Tracy laughed. "Average play, if you ask me," she said.

"It's a great one for him," Jeremy said. "Remember how he was at the first of the season? He used to drop more than he caught."

Mr. Corrigan was still making a lot of noise. As the Scrappers ran toward the dugout, he yelled, "Now get up there and *smack* one, Chad." Chad was about to lead off in the bottom of the fourth.

The players filed into the dugout. No one commented, but everyone glanced toward Mr. Corrigan and smiled.

Chad stayed outside the dugout, and he found the bat he liked in the bat rack. But he kept looking away from his father. Finally, he turned toward the players and said, "Does anyone know who that guy is? I've never seen him before."

Everyone laughed, and Chad probably felt better for loosening things up a little. But he still had to feel the pressure when he walked to the plate. His dad kept right on shouting.

Adam was making some noise of his own. He stood at the fence and shouted, "All right, Chad. Let's put these guys away. Come on, let's *murder* them. Right now."

Chad dug in and got ready. "Do it this time, Chad. Show what you can do," his dad called out. He didn't say, "And prove you deserve to be in the starting lineup," but all the Scrappers— including Chad—knew that was exactly what he meant.

But Jackson was mad. His face was sweaty and red. Adam could see that he was ready to get back at someone—and Chad happened to be the guy who was up.

The first pitch was way high—*wild* high. The catcher jumped for it and missed, and the ball smacked into the backstop with a huge pop. "Good eye, Chad," Mr. Corrigan bellowed, and everyone in the bleachers, as well as both dugouts, laughed.

Even the ump glanced around and smiled.

But that didn't stop Mr. Corrigan. He kept up the noise as the next pitch came in high and hard. It was ball two, but it hadn't missed by much.

Chad stepped out of the box for a moment, and Adam could see how nervous he was. Adam yelled almost as loudly as Mr. Corrigan, "Come on, Chad. You can hit Jackson. We *all* can."

Jackson glanced toward Adam, and then he looked back to the plate. He fired a pitch that pounded into the catcher's mitt. Chad didn't even move.

"Strike one!" the umpire called.

The next pitch was a repeat of the last one, and Chad may have flinched a little, but he didn't swing. His dad was now yelling, "Get that bat off your shoulder, Chad. You can't hit the ball if you don't swing."

Chad listened too well. The next pitch was high again, well out of the strike zone, but Chad went up after it and missed it clean.

Strike three.

Adam felt sorry for the kid, but he was also a little ticked at him. If the Scrappers were going to put the Stingrays away, they needed to get something going.

Chad walked slowly back to the dugout. He looked defeated. At least his father had finally shut up. But then Adam glanced up to see the man climbing down from the bleachers. He walked beyond the dugout to the fence that ran down the left field line. "Come here, Chad," he commanded.

Chad walked over and stood before his dad. Mr. Corrigan wasn't yelling now, but his voice was easy to hear. And he really worked Chad over. "The other kids didn't let that pitcher scare 'em. What's wrong with you? Are you afraid to get in there and battle against a big guy like that?"

When Coach Carlton saw all this, he walked over. He was about to say something when Mr. Corrigan saw him coming and ended the conversation.

Chad glanced at the coach, but he said nothing, and when he walked back to the dugout, he didn't look at anyone. Maybe he had been able to joke before, but there was nothing funny about this.

Adam wasn't laughing either. Robbie was coming up, and Adam wanted him to crunch one. "Jackson is *nothing*," Adam yelled. "Blast one out of here."

Robbie wasn't frightened—not like Chad—but Jackson had some confidence now. He was really gunning the ball, throwing even faster than before. Robbie swung a little late on a pitch and bounced a ground ball to the first baseman.

Adam was furious about that. He wished he were still in the game himself. He wanted to hit another homer.

But Gloria only managed a weak grounder, and the inning was over, the side retired in order.

Adam crashed on the bench. "What's going on?" he said. "How can we tee off on this guy in the first inning—and then do *nothing* after that?"

"Hey," Tracy said, "chill out. The score is ten to one. What are you worried about?"

"I'm not worried. I just don't want to let up on these guys."

"What's gotten into you?" Jeremy said. "You're out for blood today."

"I just want to win, like everyone else," Adam said, and he was angry that he had to explain that. He wanted to say, "Some of you guys think I'm not loyal to the team, but I am."

Tracy laughed. "You're the guy who usually forgets there's a game going on. Now, all of a sudden, you're Mr. Cheerleader."

"Hey, why not?" Adam stood up and looked down at Tracy. "I give one hundred percent, all the time. And don't ever say I don't."

"All right. All right." But Tracy was laughing. "You're still uptight about this thing with your cousin, aren't you?"

"No. I'm just . . . you know . . . hoping to get a win today."

What Adam knew was that Tracy was right. He needed to calm down. Yet it bothered him that kids had been talking and some of them thought he might go easy on Stan.

But Adam had to let all that go. He sat down, calmer. The Stingrays weren't very likely to come back from nine runs down. There really wasn't anything to worry about.

Mr. Corrigan was still barking orders to his son. "Poor Chad," Jeremy said. "I feel sorry for him."

Adam was surprised. "What about that stuff Chad's dad said about you the other day?" he asked. "Aren't you mad about that?"

"Not really. He's just a dad who wants his kid to play."

"But everything he said was untrue. You're a good player."

"I mess up in the outfield more than Trent or Thurlow do."

"Earlier in the season you did. But not very often anymore."

"We all mess up sometimes," Tracy said.

"I cost us a game, though."

"No," Adam said. "You know what the coach always says about winning together and losing together. I made some bad pitches in that game, so it was just as much my fault we lost as it was yours."

"I dropped a ground ball," Tracy said. "That's what got that last inning off to a bad start."

Jeremy looked down at the dirt, at his feet. "I thought everybody was mad at me," he said.

"No way."

Jeremy nodded, and Adam liked the way he felt.

As it turned out, Ollie ran into a little trouble in the fifth inning. He walked a couple of guys to start the inning and then gave up some hits. The Stingrays ended up with three runs. But then the Scrappers came alive and got a couple of runs themselves in the bottom of the inning. And that was the score as the game went to the seventh inning: 12 to 4.

Adam was still sort of disappointed. He felt like the team had let up after that first inning. He had the feeling that if he had stayed in the game, he would have knocked another long one. He was a fighter—a scrapper—and no one could say otherwise.

CHAPTER SIX

All the Scrappers needed now was to get the Stingrays out one more time. Adam hoped Ollie would get tough and get them quickly. Petey Peterson was up to bat again. He and Wilson were good friends. When Petey approached the batter's box, Wilson made some sort of comment, and both guys laughed.

Adam wasn't sure he liked that. Maybe that kind of stuff was okay after a game, but in the heat of the battle, guys shouldn't be swapping jokes.

"Let's go," Adam yelled. "Come on, Wilson. Let's put these guys out of their misery."

Petey stepped to the plate, and suddenly he looked all business. He took a good cut at the first pitch and fouled it into the dirt. Then he let a pitch go by for a ball.

Ollie came back with a mean fastball at the knees. Petey was off balance when he swung, but he got his bat on the ball and bumped a little fly toward right field. It was not hit well at all, and it was dropping fast as Chad charged toward it.

Adam thought that Chad would have to pull up and take the ball on one hop, but at the last second he dove for it. For a moment, Adam wasn't sure whether he had made the catch, but Chad jumped to his feet and held his glove in the air.

This time Chad really had made a great catch!

Chad raced toward the infield as though he had forgotten there was only one out. But then he tossed the ball to Cindy and yelled, "One away." He looked like he had just made a fantastic catch in the seventh game of a World Series, not in a 12 to 4 game in Wasatch City, Utah.

But his face was all lit up with joy, and Adam was happy for him.

And then his father, who had been yelling, "Way to go, Chad," suddenly howled, "You're great. Now you're showing what you *can* do."

Adam saw Chad's face change, saw the sudden embarrassment. He spun around and trotted back to his position.

Adam felt like climbing into the bleachers and telling Mr. Corrigan what a dimwit he was—and what he was doing to his son. He knew he couldn't do that, of course, but someone needed to. Poor Chad had just made his best play of the year, and his dad had taken it away from him.

The Stingrays kept battling. They were all yelling that they could still win the game. They just needed to get a rally going.

The Scrappers were all making fun of that idea, but Elise took a fastball and then timed one of Ollie's curves. She poked the ball up the middle for a single. Then she ran hard, made the turn, and bluffed a move to second before she decided to stay at first.

Adam liked that. She wasn't giving up. She was staying aggressive out there. That's how baseball was supposed to be played.

Reynolds came up then, and he had the same attitude. He bounced a ground ball to the left side. He didn't hit it hard, but it seemed to have eyes. Robbie broke to his left from third base and stretched hard, but the ball was just beyond his reach.

Gloria made the same move to her right, but she couldn't get to the ball either. It rolled into left field, and the Stingrays had two runners on.

Elvin Badger came up with a chance to keep the rally going. But he didn't use his head. He swung for the fence every time and finally struck out on a pitch that was up at his eyes.

That brought up a pinch hitter, a guy named Walters. He was the Stingrays' last hope, but he didn't look like much of one. He was a skinny kid with a weird, bent-over stance. He watched as Ollie threw a couple of pitches that missed the outside corner. Then he finally reached for one that was probably ball three. He hit a fly ball to right.

Adam held his breath. Chad had done well today, but sooner or later, he usually messed up if he got enough chances. He did misjudge the fly a little and was late getting back on it, but it was hit very high, and he finally stationed himself under it, reached up, and grabbed it.

Three chances, three catches. Chad had to feel good about that, and all the players made sure they let him know. He got almost as much praise and attention as Ollie did.

The Scrappers and Stingrays each huddled up to give the other team a cheer, and then they lined up to slap hands. Adam could see that the Stingray players had saved some pride and felt pretty good about themselves. They had taken a hard beating in the beginning, but after that, they had stayed tough. Adam had to admire them for that.

The coach didn't call the kids together this time. He merely shouted to them, "See you at the next practice."

Adam was ready to head to his bike when he heard a loud voice not far away.

"You saw what he did out there today. He's playing better and better, don't you think?"

Coach Carlton was standing near the dugout. He was looking down, putting bats into his equipment bag. "He certainly is, Mr. Corrigan," he responded. But Adam could hear a hint of frustration in the coach's voice.

"Don't you think he's ready for a start?"

Adam couldn't believe this. He looked around to see that Chad was curling into himself, his shoulders hanging, his head down.

"Mr. Corrigan, Chad has come a long way. You have a right to be proud of him. But all of our players are getting better." The coach had stuck the last bat in his bag. He picked it up and turned to walk away, but he stopped when Mr. Corrigan persisted.

"You can't tell me that he isn't as good as that little kid you have in center field most of the time. Today he earned the right to start ahead of that guy. Did you see those catches he made?"

Coach Carlton turned and faced the man squarely. He paused for a moment, probably to get his anger under control. He said, quietly, "Mr. Corrigan, Chad started the season way behind most of the players. He's still not as skilled as most of the other kids. That's why he hasn't started a game so far."

Mr. Corrigan's face was hard and set. "Do you think I don't have eyes to see what's going on out there? You're playing favorites—and I don't know why."

"That is not true, sir. I think Chad would be the first to tell you, he's hitting somewhat better, but he still isn't the hitter that Jeremy is. You know that yourself. He made some good catches today, too, but he doesn't have the speed that Jeremy has, and he still—"

"You've just got your mind set against him. You're destroying his confidence. He hardly dared swing today, he's so afraid he won't get a hit every time up."

The coach stood for a time, just shaking his head. By now a lot of people, both players and parents, had stopped what they were doing and were listening to the conversation. "Mr. Corrigan," Coach Carlton said, "if anyone is hurting your son's confidence, it's you. If you don't stop yelling at him all the time, and—"

"You don't know what you're talking about. You—"

"Dad!"

Mr. Corrigan looked down at his son. He seemed shocked. For a few seconds, all was silence.

"Stop it. That's enough. I'm not as good as Jeremy. I'm not as good as most of the players. But so what? I haven't played much before this year. Coach is helping me get better, and I like playing on this team. So leave him alone." Then he added, softly, "And leave me alone."

Chad walked away, heading toward the bike rack. All the while he was working the combination lock, his father just watched, and no one said a word. Finally, Chad got on his bike and rode away. By then most of the other parents and players were walking away as well, allowing Chad to escape all the attention.

But Mr. Corrigan turned back to the coach. "Those are the ideas you've put into his head. How can he ever be any good if he doesn't believe in himself?"

The coach stepped closer to Mr. Corrigan. "Sir," he said, "that is a fine boy. He's working his head off to learn this game. Every time you embarrass him with that foghorn voice of yours, I feel like asking you to leave and never come back. He's your son, not mine, but you better start treating him with some respect, or he'll never respect you."

Mr. Corrigan, for once, was speechless. He stared at Coach Carlton for a long time before he mumbled something that Adam couldn't hear. Then he left.

Adam heard Robbie's dad say, "Coach Carlton is exactly right. I'm sure glad he told that guy the truth. Someone needed to."

"Yeah, but will he listen?" Robbie asked.

"Probably not," Mr. Marquez admitted.

CHAPTER SEVEN

When Adam got home after the game, he showered and put on his swim trunks under a pair of shorts and a T-shirt. Then he rode his bike back to the park. By the time he got there, the Pit Bulls and the Mustangs were in the fourth inning. The Pit Bulls were holding their own, too. They were only behind 3 to 4.

Adam spotted some of the Scrappers, who had hung around after the game to see whether the Mustangs might happen to lose a game. Wilson and Thurlow were there, and so were Robbie and Trent.

Adam walked over and sat down next to them. "Hey, do you think the Pit Bulls can beat these guys?" he asked.

"It looked that way at first," Robbie said. "The Mustangs had Pingree pitching, and he gave up the three runs in the first two innings. But the Mustangs' coach brought Salinas in, and he's shut them out ever since."

"How's Egan been doing for the Pit Bulls? I didn't know he could pitch."

"He's been pretty good," Wilson said. "But the Pit Bulls have been lucky. For one thing, Flowers and Mauer are both at scout camp this week. They'll be back with the Mustangs next week when they play us, though."

Adam didn't want to mention Stan, but Thurlow said, "Your cousin is having a hard time. He's already struck out twice."

Adam nodded.

"He leans too far forward, on his front foot," Thurlow said. "Then he tries to rock back before he strides. He ends up with his front shoulder hiked up too high, and he can't get a level swing that way."

Again Adam nodded, but now he wondered what Thurlow was saying. Was he telling Adam that he ought to tell Stan that? Or was he saying, "That's between us; don't tell him"?

Adam tried again to think what he should do. Maybe he could wait until after the game with the Pit Bulls, and then he could try to help Stan. The only problem with that was, they would play each other again, later in the season.

Trent laughed. "The way Stan swings the bat, you better whiff him every time," he said. "If you don't, we'll know something's not right."

"Hey, I'll guarantee you right now, he won't get a hit off me," Adam said, and he realized his voice was much more intense than it needed to be.

Trent just laughed again.

Snake Stabler was up to bat. He hit a grounder to Stan, who was playing second base. Stan made a good pickup on the ball and flipped it to first for the out.

"Stan isn't a bad athlete," Robbie said. "He's just lost all his confidence when he's up to bat. He tries to hold out for a walk, and he gets behind in the count. Then he starts swinging at bad pitches."

That was something else Stan needed to know. But once again, should Adam tell him?

As it turned out, the Mustangs got three more runs in the fifth and pushed their lead over the Pit Bulls to 7 to 3. Lanman did knock one out of the park with a runner on in the seventh, but it was too little too late. The Mustangs ended up winning again, 7 to 5.

Stan had gotten up to bat one more time, but he got behind in the count—just the way Robbie said that he did—and then he swung at a high pitch and popped it up. The catcher had had to make a pretty good play to get to it, but that was that. At least Stan hadn't struck out.

The important thing was, the Mustangs had still only lost one game in the second half—and that was their loss to the Scrappers. The Scrappers had lost two, counting their forfeit. Someone needed to knock off the Mustangs again, and the Scrappers just couldn't lose any more.

After the game, Adam and Stan rode their bikes to Stan's house, and then they headed for the swimming hole. The water in the creek came off the snowpack on the high peaks of the Wasatch Range. No matter how hot the air was outside, the water in the stream was shockingly cold when the boys first dived in. But they were used to that, and Adam liked the way it brought him back to life after a long, hot day.

The boys eventually sat in the sun on a big

rock and let the hot air dry them. After a time, Stan finally mentioned the subject that Adam had decided to avoid. "I don't know whether anyone told you," he said, "but I didn't get a hit again today. In fact, I struck out twice."

"Is that right?" Adam said. He didn't want to admit that he had talked to the other guys about Stan's hitting.

"I don't know what's going on. At first I thought I wasn't concentrating. But now, I'm thinking *too* much. I've got myself all psyched out."

"Once your confidence gets shot, it's hard to get going again," Adam said. Then he tried to think whether it would be all right to give him a few hints. "Are you going up to bat thinking you want to get a walk?"

"Not exactly. But the coach always says we should make the pitcher throw strikes. I guess maybe I hope for a couple of balls, and then the pitcher will have to groove one."

"That's true, but if you take good pitches and get behind, then the pitcher has the advantage."

Adam had said about as much as he felt comfortable saying. He felt like he was already on the border of revealing the stuff Robbie had talked about. If Adam wasn't careful, he would start telling Stan to shift his weight to his back foot. He felt like he just couldn't reveal that kind of stuff without double-crossing his team.

"Are you still going to throw me some pitches?" Stan asked.

"Well, yeah. I guess so."

"When?"

"One of these days."

"How about tomorrow?"

"Okay. I'll just throw you some pitches—and give you a little extra practice."

"That would really help, Adam."

"But listen, Stan. When I face you in the game, I'm going to do everything I can to get you out. If I throw you some batting-practice pitches between games, that won't show you any of my real stuff."

"I've seen your stuff. You're tough."

"Sometimes, Stan, but I'm like everyone else. I have some really bad days. You're just in a hitting slump right now. You'll come out of it."

"Maybe. But I'm thinking I might drop out

of baseball after this year. In fact, I might quit sports. I'm just not that good."

"Come on, Stan. We're going to play on teams together in high school. We've always talked about that. Don't give up on yourself now."

Stan shrugged, but he didn't tell Adam what he had told his own father—that he knew Adam was better at sports than he was. And once again, Adam had to wonder: *What would it hurt to give Stan some pointers about what he's doing wrong?*

On the following morning, Adam and Stan got together at the park, and Adam threw pitches while Stan tried to improve his swing.

"So where am I messing up?" Stan asked, after a time.

It was about 10:30, and warm, but not as hot as it would be in a couple of hours. Adam took his hat off and wiped the sweat from his forehead. "I'm not exactly sure. It's hard to tell from here, but you look pretty good. Try a couple more. Focus on the ball. Watch it all the way in to the bat."

That was normal advice—something anyone

would tell him. Adam could see no harm in that.

Stan set up again, took a hard swing, and missed.

Adam could see what Thurlow had talked about. Stan was shifting his weight back and forth, getting off balance. But what was Adam supposed to say? He kept throwing, but he didn't tell Stan what he thought was wrong.

And then he heard a voice from behind him. "You're not swinging level. You've got your left shoulder way up in the air."

Adam knew the voice. He turned around, and sure enough, it was Coach Carlton. The coach walked on by Adam and approached Stan. "Take your stance," he said. When Stan did as he was told, the coach stepped in front of him. "Where do you have your weight?" he asked.

"I don't know."

"It's too much on your left foot. Shift your weight back." He watched and then said, "Okay, that's better. When Adam throws the ball, don't throw your weight back and then forward. Hold it back until the ball comes, and then stride into the ball. Keep those shoulders steady and level. You were ending up with the bat way down and your front shoulder up in the air."

The coach had Stan take some phantom swings, without a pitch. And for a time, he just worked with him, helping him keep his shoulders level. Then he said, "Go ahead, Adam. Throw him a pitch now."

Adam nodded, but this seemed like a very strange thing to be doing.

Stan took his stance, with his weight balanced more on his right foot. His swing looked better, but the motion was obviously new to him. He swung over the ball the first few times he tried.

"Just watch the ball to the bat now," Coach Carlton told him.

And then, *crack!* he caught one on the nose.

"All right!" Stan said.

Coach Carlton laughed. "Feels better, doesn't it?" he said. He turned to Adam. "A little faster this time. Make him work for this one."

Adam let loose with a good fastball. Stan swung and missed.

But Adam kept throwing, and the coach kept reminding Stan about his balance, his stride.

Stan started to connect on some of the pitches. After he stroked a line drive to left, he grinned and then thanked the coach.

"Hey, go chase that one," Adam said. "I've run out of balls."

Stan took off, running hard, like he loved the idea that he had to run a long way to get the ball.

Adam took the chance to walk over to the coach. "I was throwing to him, but I didn't think I was supposed to tell him anything that might help him," Adam said. "Are you sure it's okay?"

"He's your friend, isn't he?"

"Yeah. And my cousin."

"Then why wouldn't you want to help him?"

"He might get a hit and beat us in our next game."

Stan came trotting back about then, and Adam thought the coach might drop the subject, but he didn't. He said, "Adam, sometimes I think you kids miss the point about playing sports. The reason for a league like this is for all of you to learn to play the game. Sure, every team wants to win the championship, but the kids who finish last ought to improve and have fun, the same as the winners."

"But don't you have to be loyal to your team?" Adam asked.

"Yes. But that means giving your full effort out there. Tell me this, when Stan here comes up to bat, are you going to try to get him out?"

"Sure."

Coach looked at Stan. "Are you going to try to get a hit?"

"Sure."

"Okay. That's what it's all about. Competition. Fun. You're swinging better now, so you've got a better chance. But that's how it should be. You should bring your best to the game, and so should Adam. It's going to be fun to see what happens. If you get the hit that beats my team, I'll slap you on the back and congratulate you. But I gotta tell you, I hope ol' Adam here strikes you out."

Stan laughed. "I probably don't have much of a chance against Adam."

"Don't say that. I've watched you play. You're a good athlete. You've really improved your infield play. There's no reason you can't be a good hitter."

"Thanks."

"What are you doing over here, Coach?" Adam asked. "We don't have a practice, do we?"

"No. I was just driving by, and I saw you two. I slowed down and watched Stan swing, and I could see what he was doing wrong. I couldn't stand to drive on by and let him keep on doing it."

"Thanks, Coach," Stan said. "You're a good guy. Most coaches in the league wouldn't have done that."

"Yeah, well, I guess I don't understand that." Then the coach said his good-byes and left.

Adam was a little ashamed of himself. Now he wished he had given Stan more help.

"What a great guy," Stan said. "I'm going to start hitting better now."

"Maybe. Maybe not. I wasn't throwing you my good stuff, you know. I've got a wicked curve and a straight change. And in a game, I move the ball around a lot more."

"Yeah, I know." Adam saw Stan lose that confident look that he had taken on, and he wished he hadn't kidded with him. At the same time, he hoped the guy didn't have a great game against him. He still worried what his teammates would think about that.

CHAPTER EIGHT

Tuesday's game was under the lights. That meant that the game would begin in the light of day but end under the ballpark lights as the sun went behind Mount Timpanogos.

Adam warmed up with Wilson, and he felt good. He was in control of all his pitches. He just hoped he could win the game without embarrassing Stan.

At dinner, Adam's dad had brought up the whole situation again. "Uncle Richard told me what you did, Adam," Mr. Pfitzer had said. "It was good of you to help Stan out, and I guess your coach was great to him."

"Yeah," Adam said. "Coach showed him some things that ought to help him."

"See. That's exactly what I've been telling you. At this level, sports are not only about winning and losing. Stan just needs some help with his confidence. I'm glad you worked with him."

But warming up now, Adam was well aware that his teammates were going to be watching to see what he did when he pitched to Stan. And Adam told himself he would go after the guy like he was the Pit Bulls' best hitter—and Adam's greatest enemy. No one would have any doubt about his commitment to the team.

"Let's get this thing started," Adam finally said to Wilson, walking over to him.

"Yeah, you're ready. So am I," Wilson said, and then he added, almost whispering, "Hey, here comes Chad."

Chad was walking away from his father, and he was shaking his head. He looked upset. As he walked up to Adam and Wilson, Adam asked, "Are you okay?"

Chad hesitated, but then he said, "Not really." He sat down and started changing into his baseball shoes.

Wilson crouched next to Chad. "Is there anything we can do?" he asked, keeping his voice soft.

"No. My dad's just on my back. He's got it in his head that I have to be some kind of star player. In the car, on the way over here, I told him that sports weren't all that important to me—that he cares more about my being good at baseball than I do. He about lost it."

"He's just pulling for you to do well," Adam said.

"No, he's not. He wants me to be a starter whether I deserve it or not. I told him never to say anything to the coach again. And to quit yelling so loud all the time. He didn't like that, I can tell you."

"Sometimes dads don't want to let their kids figure things out for themselves," Adam said, but he was thinking more of his own father than he was of Mr. Corrigan.

The umpires were calling for the Scrappers to take the field. The coach called the kids together first and gave them the batting order—with no changes from the last couple of games. And then Adam walked out to the mound and took his final few warm-up pitches.

The ump called for the Pit Bulls' leadoff batter. Waxman. Adam remembered this guy. He was a decent hitter, but his real strength was his speed.

Adam definitely wanted to set the tone early—send the Pit Bulls the message that he was in charge of this game. He started with a good fastball down and in. Waxman took it, and it was close, but the umpire called it a strike.

Adam came with his curve. It was in tight, and Waxman was leaning away as it broke over the plate. Strike two.

Now Waxman would be looking for a heater, so Wilson called for another curve. This one broke outside, but Waxman chased it and missed.

"Strike three—yer out!" barked the ump. Adam felt a thrill of satisfaction. Three pitches, one away, and his first K for the night. Adam loved pitching when he could control the ball that way.

"Atta way to do it," shouted Robbie.

"Keep 'em coming," Gloria yelled.

James Wayment came up next, looking very intense. Adam loved it when he watched the guy get gunned down by Gloria on an easy hopper.

Next came Lumps Lanman. He was a big, chunky guy, but he could really damage a baseball. Adam threw a fastball, a little outside, and hoped that Lanman would get too eager. But Lumps laid off the ball.

Wilson signaled for a change-up, and Adam liked the idea. He palmed the ball but threw with a full motion. The ball drifted toward the plate, and poor Lanman started his swing way too early. He did manage to make contact, but he pushed a grounder down the first base line. Ollie ran up and fielded it, and then he tagged Lanman.

It was a great start. Adam knew he had never pitched better. As he walked to the dugout, he heard the cheers, and his teammates slapped him on the back. What he liked best, though, was that he wasn't scared and worried. He felt focused on the game, and he wasn't tempted to drift off into his own fantasies.

Jeremy looked eager as he grabbed a bat. Adam suspected that he had something to prove—especially to Mr. Corrigan.

Wayment was pitching today, not Tony Gomez, the guy the Scrappers had faced twice before. The word was that Wayment was stronger than Tony, with a better fastball, but not much else. If the Scrappers could get timed in on his speed, the way they had with Jackson, they should be able to handle him.

Wayment showed Jeremy his fastball right off. And it definitely had some pop to it. It got past Jeremy before he could trigger.

Jeremy fouled a couple off, but then he swung and missed for strike three. Maybe Wayment wasn't going to be a soft touch after all.

Adam told Jeremy it was okay, but Jeremy looked disgusted with himself as he walked back to the dugout. Adam thought he saw him take a quick glance at Mr. Corrigan, who was sitting in his usual spot at the top of the bleachers. At least he wasn't yelling . . . yet.

Robbie was ready for Wayment's fastball. He went with an outside pitch and punched it over the second baseman's head for a single.

Gloria wasn't scared either. But she hit a line drive right at Dave Boone, the shortstop. She almost knocked him down with the shot, but he held on. Two away.

Thurlow hadn't hit a long shot for a while. Adam hoped he would do it now. But he hammered another one at Boone, this one a hard grounder. And Boone was up to it again. He took the ball on a flat hop, caught his balance, and flipped the ball to Stan, who made the putout at second.

Adam had been hoping for another laugher, like the game with the Stingrays. But no such luck. The Pit Bulls looked tough today.

All the same, Adam kept his mind on the business at hand. When he went back to the mound in the second inning, he got ahead in the count to Krieger, a lefty, and then struck him out on a curve that broke in on his hands.

Boone fouled off three in a row, but then he got around on the pitch and smacked it into the gap between short and third. Gloria chased it and managed to knock the ball down, but she couldn't make a clean stop. Boone was on.

Tony Gomez came up next. He was playing first base today. He was not a slugger, but he got on base a lot by spraying little line drives around the field. He could be overpowered, though, so Adam stayed with his fastball and busted some unholy shots over the plate at the guy's knees. Gomez fouled a couple off, but he never put the ball in play. He finally struck out when—after all the hard stuff—Adam surprised him with a change-up.

Two outs.

Adam loved the frustration he saw on Gomez's face when he slammed the ground with his bat and then marched back to the dugout.

Wilson trotted out to the mound. Adam didn't know why. Things were going well.

"Tony is so cocky. I love to put him away," Wilson said. "You're pitching great."

"Thanks." But Adam waited. What was this about?

"Are you ready to take on Stan now?"

Adam had kept his focus entirely on Gomez. He hadn't even noticed Stan in the on-deck circle. "Sure," he said. "Why wouldn't I be?"

"Let's get him. Let's strike him out."

"You don't need to psych me up to do that. That's exactly what I intend to do."

"All right. Great." Wilson ran back to the plate and got ready. He called for a fastball and set the target on the inside edge. Adam knew what that was about: blast one in close, and put a little fear in Stan.

Adam nodded, but then he took a quick look at Stan. He looked scared already.

Adam kicked and fired hard, but he missed his target and got the ball out over the plate. Stan let it go by, though, and the umpire called it a strike.

Adam couldn't believe how lucky he had been. He had given Stan a good pitch to hit—way too good.

Wilson called for another fastball, and this time he set the target low. But Adam was pumped. He forced the pitch a little, and it came in higher than he intended. The pitch was belt high and down the middle again.

Stan took a good stride, on balance, and a level swing. But he fouled the ball into the dirt. Strike two.

Adam took the throw back from Wilson, then stepped to the back of the mound and looked out at the mountain. He knew he needed to settle down and control the ball. A lot of hitters would have blasted that last pitch.

But he wasn't going to feel sorry for Stan. One more good pitch, and he could put him away.

Wilson signaled for another fastball, but Adam wondered about that. It was time to cross Stan up, change speeds on him the way they had done with Lanman and Gomez. So he shook off the sign until he got the signal for a straight change. Then he cupped the ball in his palm and fired away.

The ball seemed to glide toward the plate in slow motion. It took forever to get there.

But Stan wasn't fooled. He seemed to know it was coming. He waited, waited, and then took that smooth stride the coach had taught him.

He drove the ball hard, straight up the middle.

It was a clean single. Jeremy charged the ball and forced Boone to stop at second, but Stan had met the challenge and won.

Adam felt strange. He wondered what his teammates were thinking. He hoped they knew he had been trying to throw Stan off—not giving him something he could hit. But he also wondered about his decision. Now he wished he'd stayed with his fastball.

When Sarah Pollick came up, Adam knew he had to put her away and not let Stan's hit make a difference in the game. He threw her an inside fastball that moved her back a little, and then he bent a curve over the plate. She mistimed the pitch and hit a comeback hopper right to Adam. He ran halfway to first and then tossed the ball underhand to Ollie.

And that was it for the Pit Bulls' at bat.

But as Adam walked to the dugout, Coach Carlton stopped him. "Why did you go with a change-up, Adam?"

"Just to throw him off. We've done that a couple of times today, and it's worked."

"Sure. But that works best with a big swinger who's starting to time you. When you've got a guy overpowered, it's best to keep firing at him."

"Yeah. I thought the same thing . . . afterward. It was a mistake."

"That's all it was, wasn't it?"

"Sure."

"All right. Good."

Adam walked on toward the bench. He took some more slaps on the back, but he also noticed some sideways glances, even some whispers. He thought he knew what some of the players were thinking.

But he hadn't given Stan a break. He knew that much for sure.

Finally, Robbie said, "Hey, I thought you guaranteed us that Stan wouldn't get a hit off you."

Adam looked Robbie in the eye, and he said, loud enough for everyone to hear, "I should have stayed with my fastball. I tried to get too tricky, and it backfired on me. But he won't get to me again. That's a promise."

He looked around and tried to read their faces, but no one wanted to make eye contact with him.

CHAPTER NINE

Wilson led off the bottom of the second inning. He swung hard at a Wayment fastball and hit a high chopper toward third. Lanman had to leap for the ball and then come down throwing. But Wilson hustled, and he beat the throw.

Then Tracy hit a grounder to the first baseman. She was out at first, but at least she moved Wilson over to second.

Trent didn't seem bothered by Wayment's power. He locked on to a good heater down the middle, and he jammed it hard into right center. The ball sailed past the center fielder and rolled almost to the fence. Trent ended up with a double.

Wilson rounded third and scored, and the Scrappers were on the board, 1 to 0.

That brought up Adam with something to

prove. He wanted to *pound* one of Wayment's fastballs over the fence—or maybe the closest mountain.

But he got way too eager on the first pitch, a fastball out of the strike zone, outside. He slashed at the ball and didn't touch it.

And then he swung just as hard at a pitch inside. He hit it off his fists and looped it in the air toward the shortstop. Boone ran in a few steps and caught the ball.

Adam tossed his bat away in disgust, and then he marched back to the dugout. He wanted to do *something* to lead his team to victory—and end any doubts that were still floating around.

Ollie, at least, played things a lot smarter. He let Wayment go inside, outside—and miss the plate—and he finally ended up with a walk.

That brought Jeremy up again. He looked serious, intent, but he also used his head. He let Wayment get behind again, and then he sat on a fastball down the pike. He drove it over the third baseman's head for a solid single, and Trent scored from second.

Now the score was 2 to 0. Adam hoped the team would explode, even with two outs, and put the game away early. But Robbie hit a pop-up, and Wayment took it himself for out number three.

For the next couple of innings, things stayed the same. Wayment wasn't overpowering the Scrappers. They were getting hits, but they couldn't get a big inning going. They pushed across another run in the bottom of the third, but the score was still 3 to 0 as the fifth inning began.

Adam had mowed down six batters in a row in the third and fourth innings, but then Gomez lucked out. He hit a soft grounder toward second. Tracy made a good stop on the ball, but she slipped as she turned to throw. The ball got away from her and flew past Ollie. Gomez ended up on second.

Now Stan was coming up for the second time in the game, and he had a chance to drive a run in. Adam told himself he wasn't going to let that happen. He took his time, took some long breaths, and got himself under control. No more bad pitches this time.

He threw a rocket of a fastball, and in a great spot, at the knees.

But Stan was ready for it. He got his bat out and met the ball. He didn't drive it, but the ball arced into right field and dropped in front of Thurlow.

The Pit Bulls' coach knew better than to test Thurlow's arm. He threw up his hands and stopped Gomez at third.

Adam couldn't believe this had happened again. No one could say he hadn't steamed the ball. Stan had just come through, that's all.

Adam didn't look at Stan, but he could hear Uncle Richard—*and* his own dad—cheering. All that made Adam a little angry. It wasn't going to happen again.

But Adam settled down, talked to himself, breathed in some good air from the mountain, and then he fanned Pollick on four pitches.

Morgan Roberts was the ninth batter in the lineup, and he was no match for Adam. He struck out without ever swinging his bat. That brought up Waxman, and now Adam had a chance to escape without ruining his shutout.

When Adam got set, he looked at Gomez, then glanced over his shoulder to check Stan. The guy was smiling and looking sure of himself.

He bluffed a little move, then laughed.

Adam didn't want to lose his concentration. He looked back at the batter. But just as he started into his windup, Stan took off. The pitch was high, a good pitch for Wilson to handle and throw, but Adam knew that Stan had gotten a good jump, and he didn't want Gomez to pull off the double steal. So Adam threw his arms in the air to stop Wilson from throwing to second.

What Stan had done made sense. He was now in scoring position. Adam had also made the right decision. It was hard to throw to second and then back home if the runner was safe at second. But now he wondered what Stan was trying to do. Was the guy trying to show *Adam* up?

That's when someone on the Pit Bulls' bench yelled, "That's right, Adam. Don't let your catcher throw your cousin out."

Adam was furious. He threw a dagger of a fastball at Waxman, and the kid bailed out. As he leaned away, his bat came around, and the ball hit it. The ball dropped into the dirt and then spun onto the infield grass. Wilson jumped out and grabbed it, and then he shot a quick throw to Ollie. The top of the inning was over.

The score was still 3 to 0, but now Adam was determined. He was going to show his cousin a few things the next time the guy stepped up to bat.

In the dugout, Adam stared everyone down, and no one said a word about the promise he had made.

Adam came to bat in the bottom of the inning, with Tracy on first. He swung so hard at the first pitch that it would have taken blind luck to make contact. The Pit Bulls worked him over for that, and Adam only got angrier. But he realized he was being stupid. He got himself under control and let Wayment waste a couple of outside pitches. Then he timed a 2 and 1 pitch and hit a blast to right field.

The ball was over the right fielder's head and up against the fence. Adam might have made it to third, but the coach stopped him at second. Tracy scored to make the game 4 to 0.

As soon as Adam stopped at second, he looked at the Pit Bulls' dugout. No one over there was talking to him now. Adam gave Stan a hard stare, but Stan smiled and nodded, as if to say, "Nice hit." Adam wanted to be mad, but it was hard to stay that way with his friend grinning at him.

What Adam wanted was to put the game out of reach now, but once again the Scrappers couldn't put the hits together. Ollie struck out, and then Jeremy pushed Adam to third, but Robbie and Gloria couldn't get him home.

As the Scrappers took the field to start the sixth, the coach made his substitutions. But he didn't follow quite his usual pattern. Martin wasn't there today, so the coach put Cindy at second for Tracy, and he sent Chad out to play left field for Trent.

Adam realized that Mr. Corrigan hadn't had a word to say all day. In fact, the guy didn't even cheer when he saw his son enter the game. Maybe he had listened to what Chad had told him and had decided not to be such a loudmouth.

Adam didn't give the situation all that much thought, however. He was still wired to throw some evil pitches and hold on to his shutout. That ought to quiet any doubts.

Adam made Wayment look bad, struck him

out on a scorching fastball at the letters. But
Lanman got a piece of the ball and, with his
power, sent a high fly to left field. Chad judged
the ball well, moved back into position, and
waited.

Maybe a breeze caught the ball. Maybe
Chad took his eye off it. Maybe . . . Who knew
what happened, but the ball dropped shorter
than Chad seemed to expect. He stuck his glove
down at the last moment and lunged at it, but it
trickled off his fingers onto the grass.

And suddenly the voice boomed off the top
of the bleachers. "Come on, Chad—you can do
better than that! You've got to catch those!"

The crowd fell silent in response. Everyone
knew that Chad had tried his best, and it was his
own dad who was working him over—just when
he needed support, not criticism. A lot of people
turned and stared at Mr. Corrigan. No one said,
"Hey, lay off your kid," but the message was
pretty clear. Mr. Corrigan sat down, and he
looked away from the people who were staring
at him.

Adam turned around to see how Chad was
reacting. He had thrown the ball back to the

infield, but now he was standing with his hands on his hips and staring at the ground. Coach Carlton called for a time-out, and then he ran to left field. He and Chad talked for a time, and then the coach walked back to his box on the third base line.

Lanman had ended up on second, after Chad's error, but when Krieger hit a bouncer to Robbie, Lumps made the stupid mistake of breaking for third, then stopping—caught in no-man's-land. Robbie threw to Cindy, covering second, who tagged Lumps out. Then Boone hit a fly to right, and Thurlow made a good run and gathered it in.

Adam still had his shutout, and even though the Scrappers didn't score in the bottom of the sixth, he still had his four-run lead as the Pit Bulls came to bat in the seventh. All Adam needed was three outs, and one of the batters was none other than Stan Pfitzer.

Gomez was up first, however, and Adam had to keep his mind where it belonged. He actually threw a pitch he wanted back: a curve that didn't really break. But Gomez was looking for hard stuff, apparently, and he swung awkwardly and knocked a one-hopper to Gloria. She scooped it up and then whipped it over to Ollie for the first out.

"All right!" she yelled. "Now put *this* guy away."

Adam glanced at her and nodded. He heard exactly what he needed. She wasn't accusing him of anything. She was saying, "I'm with you. You lost him twice, but let's get him this time."

But Adam was way too pumped. He let loose with a wild pitch, way over Wilson's head. Maybe it was a bad pitch, but it was also a message: Look out for cannonballs! Now Adam was going to control his emotion and pitch smart. He threw a hopping fast pitch, in close. Stan triggered and swung through it.

Adam took a long breath. He looked toward the mountains and concentrated on the pitch he wanted to throw. Wilson was calling for a curve, and Adam wanted to make Stan look a little silly.

Adam released the ball with the perfect snap, and the ball broke like it was falling off a table. Stan was completely fooled. He took a pitifully weak swing and missed.

Stan caught his balance and then looked at

Adam. He smiled and nodded, as if to say, "Now *that* was some kind of curveball."

Adam felt his attitude change. He liked his cousin's attitude, liked the fun of the two of them out there dueling with each other.

So Adam nibbled at the outside corner with a hard fastball and tried to get Stan to chase one. Stan was smart enough to lay off the pitch. Adam had to respect that.

He watched Wilson move the target back inside, and he liked the idea. But he needed to catch some of the plate and not end up with a full count.

So Adam drilled a fastball at the target, right on the inner edge of the plate.

Stan took a hard, level swing. A beautiful swing.

And missed.

It was strike three, but for a moment, Stan didn't walk away. He smiled, and he nodded to Adam, as if to say, "You got me good that time, cuz."

Adam nodded back at him, and they both laughed.

Pollick came up. She was the last chance for

the Pit Bulls. Maybe Adam relaxed a little too much, but he threw her a fastball that she hit well. She slammed a line drive to left, toward the corner.

Adam looked out to see Chad running as hard as he could. The guy didn't have a lot of speed, but the ball was staying up, and he was running all out. Just when it looked as though it would drop over him, he lunged, and he caught the ball in the webbing of his glove.

The game was over.

"Nice catch, Chad!" Coach Carlton shouted, and he jogged out toward him. "Way to polish things off for us."

Adam knew that the coach wasn't usually this loud in his praise, but he was sending a message not just to Chad but to the voice in the bleachers.

The teams huddled up then and gave each other a cheer before they walked by each other and slapped hands. The coach didn't worry about any speeches; he just sent the kids on their way. Families started piling into cars to head for home or ice-cream shops or pizza parlors. But all the Pfitzers—both families—

ended up together by the dugout.

Adam walked back to the dugout to change his shoes just as Mr. Corrigan, who had been waiting for the crowd to clear, walked over to Coach Carlton. They were standing just outside the dugout, so Adam ducked his head, but he could hear everything.

"Coach," he said, "I want to thank you for not pulling Chad after that error."

"Why would I pull him? Everyone makes mistakes."

"Yeah, I guess that's right. Anyway, thanks, and I'm sorry about . . . the things I said the other day."

"That's all right," Coach said. "It may be none of my business, but I think Chad would like to hear the same thing."

"I know. I need to have a talk with him."

"Good. I'll see you at the next game."

Adam watched as Mr. Corrigan walked toward Chad, who was talking to Cindy. Adam could see how happy Chad was about the big catch he had made.

Adam walked over to his family. Stan had just returned from his own dugout.

"Hey, cousin, you made me look bad that last time," Stan said. He was grinning from ear to ear.

Adam laughed. "I'll tell you what, Stan," he said. "You're no easy out. I can't wait for the day when we can play on the same team."

"Now *that* sounds great," Stan told him. "I'd really like that."

About then Gloria called to Adam, "Great game. Way to pitch."

Adam was glad his teammates knew where his loyalties were. Adam was a Scrapper—all the way.

TIPS FOR PLAYING FIRST BASE

1. Most first basemen are tall, and many are left-handed. But most important, you need good hands. You're an infielder, but you will also catch more thrown balls than anyone on the team except for the catcher. If you are left-handed, think about playing this position. The throw to second or third is usually easier for left-handers.

2. With no runner on first, the first baseman sets up several feet inside the first base line and several feet behind the bag.

3. As the pitcher gets ready to throw, keep your weight on the balls of your feet and keep your glove low. The ball can get to first base fast, and you may not have much time to react. If you see the batter square to bunt, charge home plate as fast as you can—unless your coach instructs you otherwise. The second baseman will cover the first base bag for you.

4. In leagues where stealing is allowed, hold a runner close to the bag. Move in front of the runner and turn halfway toward the pitcher with your right foot touching the bag. Show the pitcher your glove as a possible target. If the pitcher goes home with the pitch, step away from the bag for a possible fielding play.

5. If you are playing off the bag and a ground ball is hit to another infielder, run to first base quickly. Straddle the bag with both feet touching it. Reach out and show the infielder a good target.

6. When a throw comes, stretch toward the ball to cut down the distance and the time. Keep the toe of one foot on the bag and step toward the ball with the other leg.

7. Always be sure you make the catch. If you have to pull your foot off the bag to reach a ball, better to do that than to let the ball get past you. If you catch it but miss the out, at least the runner has to stay at first. On a bad throw, try to get in front of the ball and at least knock it down.

8. If a ground ball is hit to you, you may not have time to run to first base to make the out. In that situation, the pitcher covers first. Throw the ball softly, leading the running pitcher. A throw at chest level is easiest to handle.

9. When an infielder makes a poor throw in the dirt, stretch for it if you can. If you can see that the ball can't be reached, you may want to step behind the bag, keeping your foot on it, and catch the ball on a longer hop. If the runner is close, of course, you'll have to dig the bad throw out on the short hop.

10. Learn to throw as well as catch. Sometimes you have to throw to one of the other bases. An accurate-throwing first baseman can be a big help to a team.

SOME RULES FROM COACH CARLTON

HITTING:

Hold your shoulders level as you take your stance. Keep them level as you swing. And swing on a level plain. Great hitters swing on the same plain as the ball, not on an up or down angle.

BASE RUNNING:

Focus your eyes on the base in front of you as you run toward it. You'll usually hit it in stride and be in a good position to take a direct route to the next base.

BEING A TEAM PLAYER:

Be a good sport. When players on another team make good plays, give them credit. Umpires are human; they make mistakes. But so do you. Don't always assume that you are right and the umpire is wrong. Accept the call and get on with the game. When you put down opponents or yell at umpires, you often destroy the spirit on your own team—and ruin the fun of the game.

ON DECK:
JEREMY LIM, CENTER FIELDER.
DON'T MISS HIS STORY IN SCRAPPERS #7: *TAKE YOUR BASE*.

Jeremy felt the Scrappers give up—lose their last bit of hope. Even if Jeremy stayed alive, Chad was coming up after him. There was no reason to expect anything good to happen.

But Jeremy was going to do something right today. He watched the first pitch closely, thought about poking it, but laid off and got the call. Ball one.

The pitch had been close, and Lou was a little angry. Jeremy liked to see that. The next pitch had some mustard on it, but it was up high, ball two.

"That's it. Way to watch," Coach Carlton called.

But Jeremy wanted a hit. The next pitch was down the center, and Jeremy took an easy swing and looped the ball to the right side. The substitute right fielder was playing back. He came running in, but the ball bounced in front of him, and Jeremy was on.

"That's the stuff!" the coach yelled. "Come on, Chad, keep it going."

But what were the chances? Even if Chad

somehow got a hit, then Martin would be at bat. With the weakest part of the Scrappers' order coming up, Jeremy needed to get into scoring position.

On the first pitch to Chad, Lou hardly gave Jeremy a look. The pitch was a strike, and Chad's hopes for a walk were not great.

Why wasn't the coach signaling for a steal? If he could get to second, he could score on a single, maybe even a throwing error. It was the best chance they had.

Jeremy led off the base and watched the coach. No signal.

Lou gave him a brief look, but then turned and fired. Strike two.

Now he had to go. It was the Scrappers' last hope. Maybe the catcher would throw the ball into center field. Anything was better than depending on Chad.

So Jeremy stretched his lead, watched for his chance to go.

Then suddenly, Lou jerked his foot from the rubber and made his move to first.

Jeremy was caught and he knew it.

He broke for second, but he had no chance. Pingree took the throw from Lou and then tossed the ball to Mauer, who put the tag on Jeremy as he slid into second.

The game was over, and the Scrappers had lost. Jeremy stayed on the ground. He didn't want to get up.